For my family – with whom
I've been truly blessed

Text and illustrations copyright © 2011 Rebecca Elliott
This edition copyright © 2011 Lion Hudson

The moral rights of the author
have been asserted

A Lion Children's Book
an imprint of
Lion Hudson plc
Wilkinson House, Jordan Hill Road,
Oxford OX2 8DR, England
www.lionhudson.com
ISBN 978 0 7459 6270 2

First edition 2011
1 3 5 7 9 10 8 6 4 2 0

A catalogue record for this book is available
from the British Library

Typeset in Temble ITC
Printed in China April 2011 (manufacturer LH06)

Distributed by:
UK: Marston Book Services Ltd, PO Box 269, Abingdon, Oxon OX14 4YN
USA: Trafalgar Square Publishing, 814 N Franklin Street, Chicago, IL 60610
USA Christian Market: Kregel Publications, PO Box 2607, Grand Rapids, MI 49501

Zoo Girl

Rebecca Elliott

LION
CHILDREN'S

No family

Alone.

At home!

Left behind

Friends

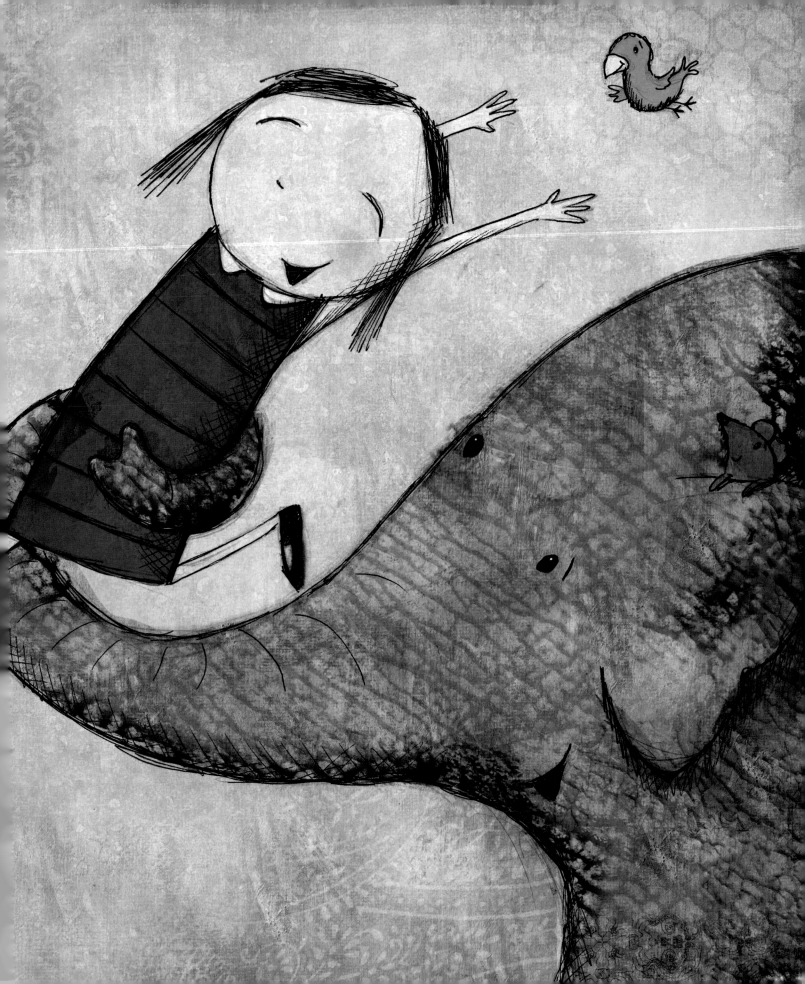

Living wild!

Discovered

A family.

Other titles from Lion Children's Books

Just Because   *Rebecca Elliott*

Sometimes   *Rebecca Elliott*

Vile   *Mark Robinson & Sarah Horne*